FEMALE PHEASANTS DON'T CALL OUT

DAVID BENNETT

ISBN: 978-1-3999-8917-6

DEDICATION

To everybody I have ever met.

CONTENTS

Acknowledgments i

Chapter 1 1

Chapter 2 6

Chapter 3 11

Chapter 4 17

Chapter 5 21

Chapter 6 24

Chapter 7 28

Chapter 8 32

Chapter 9 36

Chapter 10 41

Chapter 11 45

Chapter 12 49

Chapter 13 53

About the Author 56

ACKNOWLEDGMENTS

My family for bringing this book to print.

CHAPTER 1

It was a lovely afternoon; the sun was giving warmth to all at the house known as the Thicket in MORTON, SUFFOLK.

Dorie, who was the new cook cum carer-housemaid and keeper of finances, had just brought out tea and cakes for all, but let us remember who was left of them all at this time.

BIG BEN had just struck in the new year of 2000. So time, as it does, has moved on. Dorie had brought out a bottle of champagne for the big day, so who was around the table?

There were the three sisters, Faith, Hope, and Grace, now all in their thirties.

Lilian, who was the actress, friend of Grace and of course Dorie the maid. As they raised their glasses, Faith said how strange it was that all five should be together at this date and time (remember these five as this story progresses).

Then suddenly, the front door bell rang.

"Who on earth is that?" said Faith.

"I'll go and see," said Lilan, "as none of you seem interested."

It was quite a distance to the front door; the bell rang again before Lilian got there. She opened the door and was struck silent with what met her eyes; it was the most beautiful male, golden brown skin, (we must remember that all three sisters and Lilian were of mixed descent) and about six feet tall with the looks of someone straight from an M.G.M. film set. Lilian was speechless.

"Please forgive me," he said, "my name is JACOB MBEBEBEE, I believe one of my sisters lives here?"

Lilian finally came to her senses and

asked him in, she was in no hurry to share her find with the others, so asked him to follow her to a lounge.

Lilian was overcome with what she had heard, she then asked "Could you please tell me about yourself?"

He then went on to tell her the story that she had heard many times from the sisters, "My father was married to Mary, the mother of my three sisters, who I'm now looking for, but while he was married to Mary, he was playing fast and loose with other women and I was born to a woman named MBEBEBEE. I have all the info if you want to see it."

Lilian still felt she had found the pot at the end of the rainbow, but said "It is time for you to meet your sisters, wait here and I will go and call them."

She asked him to be patient as she may be some time, and it did take time for all to get over the shock and work out what to do. Finally, they all came to see.

The girls were still sure he was a hoax,

"But we must know more!" Faith said, "He can't stay here."

Lilian said "I have booked him in to Everard's Hotel for the time being."

Lilian took him to BURY ST EDMUNDS and booked him in. Before she left the hotel, she made a call to a friend in the SUFFOLK CONSTABULARY, they had checked his passport, and soon came back with the news; his story was genuine.

By the time the girls had decided what to do, he was well ahead. With some help from Lilian, he had found a small flat in town - and a job as a porter at the West Suffolk Hospital. Faith and Grace were both against this, but Lilian could not get enough, he was the type of man who could turn on the charm where and when he wanted. He had also joined the new church that had sprung up in Bury just known as the FREECHURCH, run by a man called Peter Shepherd. What was new about this church? They all he believed that THE HOLY SPIRIT fell on them all as in ACTS Chapter 2 in the New Testament, and all were baptized in

THE HOLY SPIRIT and spoke in other tongues, and of course, Jacob had this gift, so he was well in. With his charm and his new work in the church, Lilian was swept off her feet and could not keep away from him.

CHAPTER 2

M.G.M. Studios had been making contact with Grace for weeks, they wanted her to play the part of MARY QUEEN OF SCOTS in a new film, ELIZABETH I. It was just a small part, just right for her, to play the part of MARY up to her execution by ELIZABETH - it would only take a few weeks, but she would be perfect for the part. Grace said yes; it was not that she really wanted to get back to acting, but it was a good way to get out of the house, and the current situation.

It was very good for Grace to be back with the acting world, and she enjoyed it more that she thought she would, and was a bit sorry when it was over.

BUT, when she got back to the Thicket, what a shock, the place was a wreck, Jacob's church had had meetings all over the house, the children had had picnics all over the gardens.

Grace got straight into her car to the new church of Peter Shepherd.

They were holding a meeting when she got there, she went straight to the front, slamming tables and chairs out of her way, and then face to face with Shepherd, and with all the voice she had said "I'll ring your bloody neck!" She shouted to the church, "Get out, what I have got to say is not fit for your ears!" The church was soon empty, Lilian and Jacob were nowhere to be found, just the pastor.

He said "I am very sorry, there is a great mistake, I was told that you had gone to live in the U.S.A. and had left Jacob in charge of the house, and we could use it as part of the Church. We are a new church, we have no money, but I will talk to Lilian and get her to put things right."

Lilian came to see Grace the next day.

"Yes, I will put all things right," she said, "but now the good news is we will soon be out of your way. We have decided to get married in the U.S.A."

In fact, Jacob had already gone ahead to New York to get ready for the big day. "I do hope you will all be able to come."

Grace said, "I must go to the office and ring up the others, you wait here."

Faith said "Not a chance! I've got enough trouble of my own!"

Hope said "No, I still think there is something not right."

Grace went to look for Dorie.

But, Dorie could not be found in the house. Grace took one more look in the kitchen and then saw propped on the table a letter. It was sealed, and on it, it said 'To LILIAN'. Grace took the letter and gave it to Lilian.

The ambulance did not take long to get from Bury to Morten, a Doctor came with the ambulance. He went straight to Lilian, she had a fallen to the ground, she was shaking from head to foot in some form of convulsion, vomiting and in a very poor way.

The doctor said "She is suffering from a very bad shock; I must get her to hospital."

The people with the ambulance quickly got Lilian loaded inside, and she was gone.

Grace was alone. Silence fell on the house. It was then that Grace saw the letter she had given to Lilian, she picked it up and read it. It said:

DEAR LILIAN,

HE IS MINE NOT YOURS,
YOU CANNOT HAVE HIM,
WE HAVE NOW GONE AWAY
TOGETHER, YOU WILL NEVER
SEE HIM AGAIN, HE IS MINE,

YOURS, DORIE

Grace sank to the nearest seat, all she could think was DORIE, DORIE, DORIE, the maid of all people.

CHAPTER 3

We now know that while Jacob was in Bury, he was telling Lilian he was spending time in his new-found church. He was in fact spending time with DORIE.

The next day Grace went to BURY hospital, she did not see Lilian as she was in intensive care, but the doctor found her. He said it was too soon, but to give him a week and he may then know what the future held for Lilian.

The next morning, Grace was trying to eat breakfast, but all she could think of was now 'What now?' Then, the phone rang; It was Lily, JOSH & JENNY's old housekeeper. She had run the house for years, only to retire due to age. It was after her that Dorie came.

Lily said "Don't try to talk, I know all you are going through, you need help and will need help, and I think I have the answer. I have a niece named ANNE. I know she is the one GOD has prepared for you to help you through this time, I want you to meet her. Don't say anything now, I will send her to you."

ANNE came the next day and said "Firstly I am sure you want to know all about me. Aunt Lily has filled me in with what goes on at the Thicket, and I think I know most of what you are going through now. I would not have come if I didn't think God is asking me to come to help. I am a Christian, I was badly let down in a romance at age of twenty, but this led me to give my life to Christ. I am a member of the FREE CHURCH in BURY. I know you will have thoughts about this considering what has just happened, but Satan will always try to destroy what God is doing. Did not Jesus say 'In all you do be careful, and let no-one DECIEVE you.'"'

Grace had NO QUESTIONS, she just said "When can you come?", followed by "I think it's time for a cup of tea."

Tea was mode and then the phone rang. It was LLOYDS BANK.

"Could we please speak to Grace Johnston on a matter of some emergency? We have some concern that you have been trying to send a large sum of money over to a Mrs. D. MBEBEBEE in the last two days."

Grace said that she had not made any payment of any kind. Grace was at this time unable to carry on.

"Give me the phone, said Anne, "I used to work in a bank, I know what to do."

Anne pushed a few more buttons on the phone pad and was soon through to the Bank Fraud department. It was soon agreed that it was a fraud, the money payment would be stopped and returned to Grace's account.

Anne said "Now that I am here, let me just have a quick look through your accounts to see if Dorie had gone off with any more."

The quick look proved that £1000 a week had been taken for the past three weeks.

Grace said "We will let her get away with that if that is all she got, it won't last them long."

Anne said she must be on her way. "Isn't it good that the GOOD LORD is watching over us."

Grace walked with Anne to her car, then said to Anne "By the way, how much was DORIE trying to take out of my bank?"

Anne looked up and with a small smile said, "Not much, only £200,000."

The week of waiting was over, so Grace made her way to Bury Hospital. Lilian was still in a private room; she had aged at least twenty years. Grace hardly recognized her.

A nurse was with her, she said they were pleased with the way she had pulled through.

"We thought we would lose her, but you must see the doctor, he will fill you in."

He said "The best thing is that she can swallow food and keep it down, that is half the battle. We know she can see and hear, but how well we do not know. She has lost the use of her left arm, but she is beginning to move her legs, but what is worse for her is she is completely incontinent and will be for the rest of her time. We have a choice, we can either put her in a home for people like her, or maybe you might like to have her home with you. We can find you a live-in nurse who with some help from you or others would be able to keep her well with all her needs met."

This was agreed, and the nurse was found and came to see Grace at the house. Her name was PRECIOUS, she was aged about 25, her family had come from the West Indies, and all she ever wanted was to be a nurse. Grace now had all she needed, with the help of Precious, a room was made ready for Lilian on the ground floor. Both Anne and Precious were living at the Thicket. Lilian, gesturing with her eyes, let it be known that she was happy to be home.

CHAPTER 4

Things were going well, the two girls got on well together. The workload was not that heavy, and Grace had time on her hands. She thought she would ring Faith and invite her over to see what was going on.

Faith said "I'm sorry but I just can't make it right now, things are better between me and Andrew, we still live together, although we don't share the same bed. He still wants to know who is Tom's father, I think the time has come when I must tell him."

Grace said "I wish you well."

Andrew, Fath's husband, left for work

as usual that morning. On leaving, he said "If it's okay, I'll be home for lunch, I must have time to get on with some office work. I'll see you about 12."

Faith spent the morning offering up a little prayer to ask for God's help if this was the right time to tell Andrew.

He was home at 12 as he said, he was busy getting papers together when he said "I must find someone to take care of all my vehicles, I've got vans and lorries and no-one takes care of them. I've got a younger brother who's got a small garage just out of town, I'm going to see him to ask if he would like to take the job on."

He left before Faith could say a word.

Andrew soon found the garage. Edward was in the office. Andrew walked straight in, Edward had his works register open, on the top was his book mark with a photo of FAITH and THOMAS. Andrew's eyes went up to the office wall, and what was on the wall - a large photo of Thomas and underneath, just two words: 'MY BOY'. Neither man said a word. Andrew, in great haste, leapt into his car and left at great speed, back to see Faith!

Faith saw the car pull up. She thought 'Now comes the end of my world.'

Andrew came in with no rush, he asked Faith to sit down and then said "AT LAST, AT LAST, I KNOW, I KNOW, it is not as bad as I thought it would be, he still has my family's blood, he is one of us, he is still our child, he is still the child of Our Family, he is one of us. WHY OH WHY did you never tell me before? I understand you wanted a child that I could not give you, and I think you have done a good thing. GOD MOVES IN A MYSTERIOUS WAY, HIS WONDERS TO PERFORM."

But Andrew could not stop the feeling of the Long Hurt that Edward had caused, he just though that Edward should not have kept the secret, that somehow Edward was laughing of him, and this thought left a black spot in Andrew towards Edward. But peace was returning over the household of Faith and Andrew.

CHAPTER 5

Grace was now at a bit of a loose end, she decided to go for a walk out in the fields. She came to the place that was once the old Thicket, where she found Colin Moles, the Farmer of the Land.

They talked for a while and then Colin said "You look a bit fed up."

Grace said she had come to a bit of a full stop in her life, and she was looking for something of interest.

Colin said, "Why don't you come with me for a day out at the Racing at Newmarket, it is the July meeting next Monday. Why don't you come with me?"

Grace said she would love to have a day out, she then went on to tell him that her uncle Josh, who bought her house at Morton, his father was Philip BLAND and they once had a stud at Newmarket.

Colin said "Oh, I know some of the BLAND family, I will see if I can find some of them for you to meet. We will leave early."

It was a grand day for Racing. Colin took her first to Moulton, to Moulton Paddocks, where there were some members of her uncle's family, but they were busy as they had a horse running that day.

Grace asked "What is its name?"

They said it was Good Boy, but they didn't think it had much of a chance.

"Never mind," said Grace, "I'll still have a pound on it."

Colin then took her for lunch at the members' tent, it was very, very crowded. Then, the big race! Colin showed her how to place her bet, but as they said, Good Boy came near to last. It was a wonderful day nonetheless.

Colin took her back to her house, as he

helped her out of the car, he held her hand and said "You do a good job taking care of people. I wish there was someone to take of me."

Grace pretended not to hear, but said "Thank you, we must do this again."

She now felt that she must go and see her sister, HOPE.

CHAPTER 6

Hope's house and church were in the sprawling village of BOXTED, about two miles from COLCHESTER. Grace went first to the house, but Hope was not there. She went on to the church, it was open, but again, no-one was there. The church had been an old school, it was surrounded by a large car park and gardens. Grace walked through the chairs and seats to the front, just before the stage. There was a low lectern for kneeling. Grace knew that this lectern was called THE MERCY SEAT.

Grace was lost, what to do? But she knelt on the mercy seat, and for the first time for many years, she began to pray -

but not softly. Her prayer came out in full voice, "Lord," she said, "I don't know if you can hear me or even if you are listening, but I need your help. There is so much before me and I am responsible for the lives of many people. LORD I am here to ask you for help."

Grace then noticed a Bible on the stage close to where she sat, she got hold of it and let it fall open and she noticed someone had underlined one of the Verses. She read what it said, and to her amazement it said 'COME UNTO ME ALL YOU THAT ARE WEARY AND HEAVY LADENED AND I WILL GIVE YOU REST'. GRACE was again amazed at how quickly God came with an answer. She read on; it said 'CAST ALL YOUR CARES UPON THE LORD BECAUSE HE CARES FOR YOU'.

Tears flowed freely down Grace's face, she put the Bible back. She knew someone or something was standing behind her, at first she could not look, but then was overjoyed to see it was her sister.

HOPE said "Let us kneel together, it is time you asked JESUS into your life to be your SAVIOUR and your GOD, to give yourself just as you are into His hands that you may know Him for good and always."

The great transaction was done, Grace would never be alone again. She turned to talk to her sister, but she was gone.

It was only two miles to the village of PARSONS HEATH where Faith lived. Faith was surprised to see her.

Grace said "I've only popped in for a cup of tea, I'm on my way home after paying HOPE a visit."

Faith said "I'm surprised you found her; did you not know she is on her way to live in America? Her church here in BOXSTED is now too big for her, she has handed it over to new leaders and she is off to join the Southern Baptists in the U.S.A. She is all fired up with the idea that we are very near to the second coming of Christ. The church in England is asleep, so she is off to where she thinks it will happen, in the Bible Belt of the U.S.A. We all wish her well. May God Bless Hope."

CHAPTER 7

All was well at the house, so Grace was off to another day at the Races. It was the last day of the flat Racing Season, so Grace asked, "What next?"

"Well, for me," Colin said, "it's the shooting season. What about you?"

"That's not for me," said Grace, "I don't want to plod around mucky fields in the rain shooting Pheasants."

Grace felt she had neglected her duty in looking after Lilian. She was pleased with Lilian's alertness, but her incontinence was much worse. This was making Lilian very unhappy and she now needed more encouragement. But, her legs were stronger and she was now able to walk a few steps, and she enjoyed a short ride out in the car. Grace picked up the phone to tell Faith all the news.

A strange voice answered and said "Faith is at the Fire"

"FIRE, WHAT FIRE?"

"Oh, didn't you know? Edward's Garage has been burnt to the ground."

But Grace was thinking more about Hope. She was always the girl at school for whom the RE teacher was not good enough – Hope knew more than that, Church was not good enough for her either, she just wanted to say what she thought. Now the church had gone to sleep, she had gone on to pastures new. She wanted to tell Hope that the sheep only follow the Shepherd, if they try to get in front, they can get lost and stumble into darkness.

But what of the Fire? The police were soon to make a big thing of it, and soon found enough evidence to prove that Andrew was responsible, although Andrew said he was in Ipswich watching

Colchester play football and could bring ample witnesses to say he was not home the night of the fire.

It was the last day of the court, but the Judge said he would wish to have both sides of the case from the two brothers. The Judge asked who would speak first, it was Edward.

He said "My Lord, thank you for this opportunity for me to speak. I know I have for a long time wrought a great wrong against my brother for which I am guilty, but I am sure you know My Lord, it was Eve who picked the fruit of the tree, but Adam who took the guilt. I do not take or hold any blame against my brother."

The Judge made note of what Edward had said.

It was Andrew to speak next; "Thank you My Lord. There are many wrongs in this case, but all wrongs do not make a right. I am able and willing to put right all I have done, if we are going to use the Bible in this case, I would ask that forgiveness may be offered and accepted by both sides. Thank you."

The Judge then adjourned court and said that the court would meet tomorrow at 10:30AM, when he would give his finding of this case.

So to the next day, the court house was full, all wanted to hear the findings of the Judge.

The Judge stood and said "I find that in this case, both men have offered and accepted forgiveness and all wrongs will be put right, so my finding is this case shall be acquitted and both men will go FREE. There is no case."

Faith made her way quicky to her car, but was caught up by Andrew.

He put his hand in hers and asked "Any chance of a cup of tea?"

Faith took booth his hands and said "Yes, and a bit of cake," for Faith and brotherly love and forgiveness put all things right.

CHAPTER 8

With the improvement of Lilian and Grace having more time, Precious had more time for her love of Gardening. Her concern was that she had no water for the Roses.

Grace said “I'm sure there was something in the deeds of the house when Josh bought it, something about the well, and that it could be used for irrigation, I’ll look it up.” Grace asked Andrew if he could come and look into it.

Andrew said he hadn't the time, but he would send Edward.

Edward came the next day. Precious was in the Garden and showed him where the well was. He soon had the top off.

He said, "There's lots of water, and it smells clean. I must go and get a ladder and tools; it could be quit a big job. I'll be on my way."

Just then, Anne called out "Tea it ready, have a cup before you go."

The togetherness of Anne and Edword was made in Heaven, more to come about them later.

Edward came the next day with ladders and took ropes and a big light and was soon down the well. He was surprised, what was in the bottom? It was on old 12-bore shotgun, whatever was it doing down the well? He got it out to the top but even with much care, the wooden stock was breaking. His only thought was to take it to HODGSONS THE GUNSMITH in BURY.

They said it was no good, all they could do was to get the rust off the barrel, mend the lock and find an old stock, then put it all together, that it would only be a MUSEUM PIECE.

What about the gun? Let us go back over 80 years to this very spot. Can you see a small boy with his father? They were leaving Morton, all their possessions were on the cart ready to move to Newmarket for a new life, all that was left was the gun.

The boy asked "What will you do with the gun?"

The father said "Before it leads anyone into temptation, I will put it down the well."

With the gun now hanging in the outhouse as a MUSEUM PIECE, Edward got on with the work, putting in a pump and getting some water for the Roses. But with only Lilian to care for, Grace had more time or her hands. She saw the house was in need of care, it needed a good lick of paint and some of the windows were in need of repairs. So, much to the joy of Anne, Edward was set to work. Precious was well aware of the growing romance with Anne and Edward. Grace still had sufficient money to keep the house going, and with the much improved walking of Lilian, she was able to take her out for more rides.

Grace hadn't seen Colin for a few days, so she made her way over to Lime Tree Farm to see him. He was getting ready for a day's shooting, but as we know Grace was not into shooting Pheasants.

Colin said "Why don't you come and have a go at CLAY PIGEON shooting? The pigeons are made of round discs of clay about four inches in diameter, they are fired up in the air and we try to hit a moving target."

Grace said she would like to have a go at that.

Colin said "We are having a shoot next Saturday, I will take you."

Grace enjoyed it very much, but Colin's gun was too heavy for her, so he said he would get her a lighter one, what is known as a number 20-bore.

"I will let you know when it is ready."

CHAPTER 9

Anne said "Colin rang, your new toy is ready, he wants you to go over and try it out." Grace could not wait.

When Grace and Lilian arrived though, there was no Colin to be found. After ten minutes, he pulled up in his Rover.

Colin said he was sorry not to be there when they came, but he was out on the farm frightening wild birds off his newly planted barley. He left his gun and cartridges in his car.

Grace had one more look out at Lilian in the car, she was sure she was okay, but with her half-open eyes, you could never really know. Grace and Colin made their way to the house. Grace soon had hold of her gun, and with the high ceilings in the old Farmhouse Kitchen, was soon making pretend shots at Clays.

"We will take it out next weekend," said Colin,

Grace said, "We have been some time, I must go back to Lilian."

Colin put the gun away and they began to make their way back. It was at the kitchen door that they heard the shot.

They ran to the cars and somehow, we will never know how, Lilian had gotten Colin's gun, loaded it, got back into the car and then with the gun between her legs and the barrels under her chin, the Force of the shot had taken the top of her head off. Grace could only run back be the house, Colin had to call the Police, Doctors and Ambulance.

We will leave out the case with all its enquiries, it was so sad for all, all the questions, who was wrong, could anyone have done better, but in the end, Grace was very pleased to hear the court say 'We make a ruling of accidental death.'

As the case was proceeding, the solicitor and funeral director for Lilian came to Grace to ask if there was any will that she knew of, as they needed a will before they could prepare for the funeral. Grace knew where to find the private belongings of Lilian. Her will set out that it was her wish that she be cremated and a family service held in MORTON ANGLICAN CHURCH, and a small stone for her ashes to he placed in the Church graveyard as near as possible to the stones of Josh & Jenny BLAND.

Her stone should have her stage name LILIAN WALSH, and under that, the Jewish word 'חג שמח', or 'YAKSHAMAER', meaning HAPPY HOLIDAY, and then under that, the verse John 3:16.

'If you have the time', it said, 'to find a stone mason who can understand and put on my stone what I have asked, it is of great importance to me. If you find the time to read though my diary, I will explain why I want this funny Jewish word on my stone. I will warn you that it may take some time.'

Grace did so.

'As you may remember, I made a film about a Jewish woman that did all she could to get Jews out of Germany before it was too late, at the end of the film I was caught and died in the gas chambers. After the film, I made up my mind to go to Poland to see one of these HOLOCAUST CAMPS for myself. There was not much left of the camp, but some part of it was kept so people didn't forget. I was shown around, the guide first took me to the big room where they were made to get ready and then made to go through the door into the gas chamber. But I was overcome by this funny Jewish word over the door, what did it mean?

I asked the guide, she said "Is this not out faith? We will all come to the last door of this life, the door that leads from life to death, or in my case, life to eternal life with my SAVIOUR JESUS. When my time comes, I shall face that last door without fear, what about you?"

I can tell you now that at that moment that little Jewish word was everything to me, because at that moment of my life I took Jesus as my SAVIOUR.'

It was later as Grace read Lilian's diary again that she realized she hadn't said 'good night' to her the previous day, just 'see you in the morning.'

CHAPTER 10

It was after the funeral that Colin came to Grace and said "You have nobody to look after now, what about me? Will you marry me?"

Grace said "I thought you would never ask," and with a hug and a kiss, plans began to be made.

They were married in the small Anglican Church in Morton, it was a wonderful day. Precious saw to it that the place was full of flowers. Anne put on the very best reception the old house had ever seen, but now all the people have gone and we are at LIME TREE FARM.

It is time.

Grace was very unsure. What next? She sat on the bed in her best nightdress. Colin came in from his dressing room dressed from head to foot in pyjamas. He came and sat on she bed and put out his hand. "Darling," he said, "I need your help. I am in my mid-thirties, I have been everywhere, done most things, but I have never known a woman."

Grace took his other hand and said "I am on my way to forty, but I can truly say I have never had a man."

Grace opened the top of her nightdress and Colin put the light out.

Colin was up and dressed before Grace opened her eyes.

Colin said "You will find me an early riser; my day always starts at 6:30AM but it has been my practice to start the day with my Bible reading and a short word of Prayer."

Grace said "If you will have me, we will keep that practice together."

Colin went off to work.

Grace was still sitting in the bed. She

picked up Colin's pillow and gave it a big hug, she thought of the night. She threw her hands in the air and said "If this is life with man and woman, BRING IT ON!"

Grace held a meeting with Anne and Precious and said there was still enough money for them to stay on. But, I feel we need to ask, what next for the house?

The next week Precious had a phone call from William Hackensforth,

"I am the General Director of M.G.M. U.S.A., could I make an appointment to see you? I would like to talk with the owner of your house."

Precious got in touch with Grace, and an appointment was made.

A large car arrived and out stepped Mr. William Hackensforth with (what we only think was) his wife. All were ready for him. He started "You all know who I am, and I believe you to be Grace Johnston, one of our stars. Well, I am here to ask if we at M.G.M. can put your house to good use, we are looking for a house like yours where we can place our old stars who have come to the end of their acting careers and are now on hard times. We want to find homes where they can end their days in love and joy and we think your home could be what we are looking for."

Edward said it would take time. "We would have to put in lifts, make changes to some of the rooms," but Grace agreed and it was done. (If we had the gift of seeing into the future, we would see elderly Ladies living in love, joy and peace, Anne as ever with cups of tea and coffee, and Precious the Mother of it all, but that's another story.)

But it was done.

CHAPTER 11

It is of no surprise that the marriage of Anne and Edward was to take place, they married at Peter Shepherd's church in Bury, just a quiet wedding.

Now Edward is full time at the Thicket, to get the house ready for its new work.

Faith came over to Morton to see Grace and to catch up on all the news. She looked at Grace and said "Married life is doing you good, you are putting on a bit of fat."

"That's not fat," said Grace, "that's the result of happy married life."

Faith said "What, not you, you're getting on for 40!"

Grace smiled and said "We are told that Abraham's wife Sarah was over ninety when she had Isaac."

Faith had a little tear come to her eye, "I always wish that I could have had a second child."

Precious came in and heard what Faith had said. Precious said "Have you ever thought of adoption?"

"Yes, but I never got around to it."

"Well, my mother is part of an organization that finds homes for unwanted children, mostly babies, but sometimes children of up to ten years old. I will get you her magazine."

Faith was sitting at the breakfast table when the postman came. It was the magazine from Precious. Without much thought, she opened it and yes, page after page, faces of Children asking for a home.

But THEN, the face of a boy, BURT.

She cried out "BURT, why BURT!"

His face just looked up at her. She read on, Father unknown, Mother known as DORIE, her second husband missing, no trace, believed to be in Spain. DORIE, now working in a London hotel, she has room for herself only. BURT is now looking for a Mum and Dad, but it was the word under the face of BURT, it just said 'PLEASE!'

Faith could do nothing for the rest of the day. Time and time again she went back to the Magazine and the word 'PLEASE!'

She left it on the table for Andrew to see.

He spent some time just looking and then said "YES, YES, YES."

Faith went back to the mother of Precious, it took some time, but at last all was okay, and Burt was on his way.

The car pulled up in front of the house, a woman got out and with her, BURT.

They were walking down the drive when Thomas broke away from Andrew, ran to Burt and said "Hello Brother."

Burt was at the Kitcher table with a

glass of Lemonade. Andrew said "Would you like another biscuit?"

"Yes please."

It was the fourth.

Thomas said "Brother you must need a wee," the two boys ran off to the bathroom TOGETHER.

CHAPTER 12

With all that is going on we have almost missed the birth of Grace's Baby. It was a girl, and though she is of an age, Grace got through the birth very well, and was soon up and about. She wanted one of those big Victorian prams, Colin called it 'the cart'.

Grace was fine, it was a nice sunny day, time she put her baby in the cart and got out in the sunshine. Grace had never looked fully around the farmyard. She found a row of small buildings, the second one was strange, the door was overgrown and it looked as if it had never been opened. The door had a small window, she tried to look through, but all she could see was cobwebs.

Colin arrived, she asked "What is the meaning of this door? Why is it shut and overgrown?"

Colin said "This door has been like this all my life, it has a very sad story. In the 1920s, Morton had a lovely young butcher named SAM, he had a very good head on his shoulders, and even had another shop in the next village. He would buy cattle from farmers that he could butcher and sell in his shops, he even bought cattle from my Uncle Tom at this farm. Uncle Tom had a daughter named ELIZABETH, they fell in love and were to marry, but Uncle Tom said

'NO, SAM came from a criminal family. Sam's father had been in Prison for poaching Pheasants' and said the wedding could not be. Sam said they would elope to France and start a new life together.

"But on the day they meant to go, he could not find ELIZABETH, at last he phoned my Uncle who said 'My daughter is locked up in her room, you will never see her again.'

"Uncle was pleased with what he had done, so with a stiff drink, made his way to bed. He thought he heard an engine running and went to find out what was going on, he came to this very spot, and yes, it was the engine of his car that was running. He opened the door and found this place full of exhaust smoke and ELIZABETH DEAD ON THE BACK SEAT. So his daughter was removed, the place was shut up, and has in my time never been opened."

Grace took his arm and said "Please, I cannot live here with this dreadful secret around me, could we not open it up and do away with it?"

Just then, two farm workers came by. Colin asked for their help, and they managed to get the door open. To their utter surprise, the place was completely empty, nothing but a hundred years' worth of cobwebs. Colin asked the men to take the door down to the fields and burn it.

Grace took hold of both Colin's hands

and said "Let us make this promise to each other, that as long as the Good Lord gives us life together, we will never have secrets."

Colin said "Never."

"And one more thing," said Grace, "if you agree, can we call our daughter ELIZABETH?"

Colin put his head in the pram and said "Hello ELIZABETH." And then, "There's a funny smell in your pram, I think our daughter needs a change."

They went into the house.

CHAPTER 13

It is a Sunday afternoon in the village of Morton, and there is a Christening service at the small Anglican church. Many of the family are there but none prouder than the mother of them all, MARY. Proud because she has been asked to be Godmother, and to give the names of the child.

Andrew is telling his two boys to stop playing about in church, but as we wait for the Vicar to come, let us just have a little look out and walk around the graveyard, where we will see the names on the many stones.

Yes, there's the first, MARY with brother SAM, and look, there's the small boy Simon with his father, you know, the man who first put his gun down the well.

And look there, a new stone, the name on it, Lilian Walsh, with her funny Jewish word that tells us of the door we must all come to at the end of this life. We wonder if the people will understand it.

But the service is about to start; we must go back in.

The Vicar asks "Who is the one who has the name for this child?"

MARY says "I DO."

"Then what are these names?"

MARY CALLS OUT in a clear voice "ELIZABETH LILIAN MARY!"

Then the Vicar takes the child and holds her over the Font, "Then by the power vested in me, I NAME THIS CHILD ELIZABETH LILIAN MARY IN THE NAME OF THE FATHER AND OF THE SON AND OF THE HOLY SPIRIT, AMEN."

AND THIS IS THE END

ABOUT THE AUTHOR

MY NAME IS DAVID BENNETT,
I am the author of these little books.

I am sure you notice I have given many of my characters a Christian Faith, you may well ask if I have a faith. The answer is yes, Jesus has been my Saviour for many years and at the age of 94, I will soon come to that last door that is either from life to death, or from life to everlasting life. I know the meaning of the word on the door, and look forward to the day when I shall walk through that door, lift my head up and say YAKSHAMAER.

THANK YOU ALL,
Good day.

Printed in Great Britain
by Amazon

48445735R00037